THE MAGIC BRACELET

Sarah and The Rainforest Rescue

Aarna Agrawal

Happy Reading!

~ Aarna

ISBN-13: 9798394162701

Cover design by: Aarna Agrawal

Library of Congress Control Number: 2018675309
Printed in the United States of America

CONTENTS

*Dedicated to Mom, Dad, my younger
brother and my grandparents.*

PREFACE

On a pleasant afternoon, Sarah and her best friend were playing in a park. Sarah was eight years old and was in third grade.

All of a sudden, out of nowhere, appeared a bracelet. It glimmered in the sun. Sarah picked it up and went home, only to find out that it was magical! She soon discovered that it can take her to places in the past, as well as the present. It also provides her with magical powers, like talking to animals!

In her first adventure, the bracelet took her on a mission to rescue dinosaurs from a volcano. In her second adventure, she finds herself underwater, and saves the animals from a sea twister.

Now, Sarah is ready to go on her third mission with her magical bracelet. Which place would Sarah journey to now?

THE GLOWING BOOK

It had been such a busy day. Sarah was exhausted as she snuggled up in her cozy bed. She grabbed a copy of her favorite bedtime story, and started reading. All of a sudden, her book began to glow! The pages turned blank, and her story disappeared. Instead, new words began forming a letter. At once, Sarah realized that her third mission was about to begin.

THE LETTER

Sarah quickly started reading the magical letter that had appeared in her book. It read,

Dear Sarah,

You have successfully completed your first two missions with the dinosaurs and the underwater sea creatures. It is now time to start your next mission. Remember, if you wish to activate a power from your magical bracelet, just clap your hands twice and say,

> *Bracelet, bracelet, I found you,*
> *Show me the magic that you can do!*

Good luck. Farewell!

-Magicland

Sarah grabbed her bracelet. Sparkles began swirling around her. She was being transported to her third mission!

THE AMAZON RAINFOREST

Sarah found herself in a beautiful rainforest, full of life. She was amazed with the strange animal sounds and plants all around her! In the distance, she noticed a small grass field next to a pond.

Just then, it had started to rain, so Sarah took shelter under a leafy tree.

"Hello. My name is Max the Monkey. Who are you?" an unfamiliar voice startled her.

Sarah looked around, but she didn't see anyone. Then, she looked up and saw a bright orange monkey waving to her. He was hanging on a branch with his tail.

"Hi, my name is Sarah." she replied. "Nice to meet you."

The rain started pouring. Max looked at the gray clouds. "We've been getting a lot of rain lately. Definitely more than usual." he said. Suddenly, thunder rumbled, and lightning struck a nearby tree, setting it on fire. Sarah watched it tumble down to the forest floor.

The fire started spreading, trapping creatures in their homes. "Oh no!" she cried. "I've got to rescue them!"

SAVING THE
ANIMALS

Sarah frantically looked around and tried to think of a way to rescue the animals. Max was nervously jumping beside her.

"What do we do?" he asked Sarah.

Suddenly, she noticed vines hanging from the trees. "That's it!" Sarah exclaimed. "You can swing on the vines and get to the other animals up on the trees. Tell them to meet me at the grass field near the pond. Meanwhile, I will take the other animals safely to the field."

Sarah and Max got straight into action. They had to make sure they rescued the animals before it was too late.

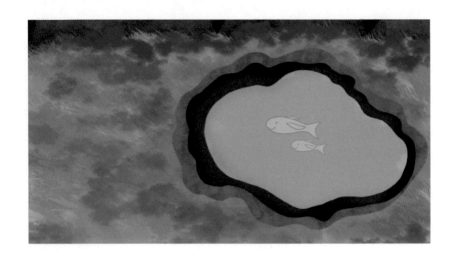

NEW HOMES

Soon, all of the animals had been rescued, and they were gathered up in a big circle on the grass field. Fortunately, the rain had put out the fire, so they didn't need to worry about it anymore.

"Is everyone safe?" Sarah announced.

"Yeah, we're fine," a snake said to her.

"But what about our homes?" a squirrel asked. "The fire burned down the trees and our homes, so now we don't have a place to live!"

Oh no! I've got to find new homes for the creatures! Sarah thought.

"Hang on, we're going to find out the best location to make new homes," Sarah assured the creatures. Then, she turned toward Max and said, "We need to find a big and healthy area of the rainforest."

"No problem," Max replied. "I have a friend named Pete the Parrot who can help us."

PETE THE PARROT

Sarah was confused. *How will Max find Pete? It was such a big rainforest. Pete could be anywhere!* she thought.

Suddenly Max yelled, "Pete, we need your help!" His loud voice boomed through the jungle. Sarah and the animals covered their ears.

How can Max be so loud? Sarah wondered. *Oh, he must be a howler monkey!*

A few minutes later, Sarah saw a parrot coming toward them. It was Pete! Max waved to him, and he came down on the ground.

"Could you help search for a good spot for these animals to make new homes?" Sarah asked him. "They need a place to live because the fire destroyed this whole area."

"Roger that," Pete squawked. He flew back into the distant trees, in search of the perfect spot.

ACROSS THE
AMAZON

Everyone was waiting for Pete and it had felt like hours had passed. All of a sudden, Sarah heard a familiar voice, and she saw bright feathers in the distance. Pete was back!

"I found the place!" he squawked. "It's an open area. We have to go north, turn left, cross the Amazon River, and then it will be just ahead!"

Max agreed. "That side of the river is even better because it's healthier and greener, so it's great for the new homes!" He said eagerly.

Sarah replied. "Great job Pete! Sounds perfect. You can take the birds with you, while Max and I will proceed with the remaining animals."

Everyone began moving. They were all excited to go to their new homes.

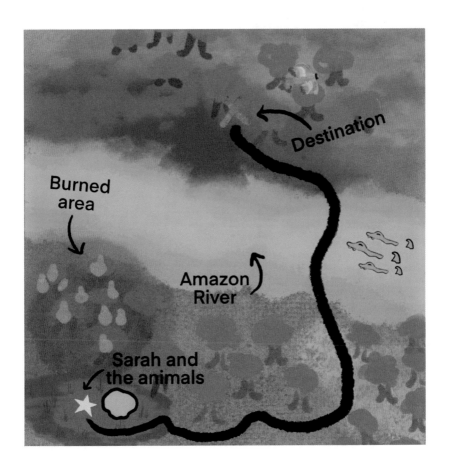

THE ALLIGATORS

After some time, Sarah and the animals had made it to the river crossing. The Amazon River was just ahead of them! It looked very deep in this area, and three alligators were resting peacefully at the river bank.

"How are we going to cross the river without waking up these alligators?" a jaguar asked Sarah. She thought for a moment. Finally, she said, "Everyone, back up. I'm going to try and negotiate with them."

As Sarah was getting closer to the alligators, Max yelled, "Watch out Sarah!" An alligator jumped at her and just in time, she pulled herself back.

"What do you want from us?" he snarled.

Sarah tried to be as calm as possible. "These animals' homes have been destroyed. We need to cross the river so that we can get to a suitable part of the rainforest," she explained. "Could you help us?"

"Fine, we'll help you. We understand that it's important for everyone in the rainforest to have a safe place to stay." He replied. "Oh, and my name is Andy."

Sarah and the others cheered! Now, they could safely cross the river.

HIGH TIDE

The alligators started helping everybody cross the river. One by one, the little animals hopped on their backs and made it safely to the other side, while the others swam. But as the last group of animals were crossing the river, a gigantic wave appeared on the horizon.

"Oh no! It's a tidal bore!" Max yelled. "A tidal bore is a strong tide traveling up the river. Everyone, hold on to something! It can sweep you away!"

They all rushed to the other side, and quickly held on to trees and branches.

A few moments later, the wave hit and the water created a big splash. Thankfully, everyone was safe, or so Sarah thought. The wave was so large that many fish were swept in the trees. They needed to be in the water soon!

"Oh no!" Sarah cried. "I have to return them back to the water, and fast!" It was time to activate a power! She clapped her hands twice and said,

"Bracelet, bracelet, I found you,
Show me the magic that you can do!"

A screen popped up and she chose the power to move objects with her mind. Sarah concentrated hard, and said, "Move these fish back to where they belong!" Soon, all of the fish were transported back in the water. "Thank you!" they said to Sarah, and quickly swam away.

Sarah and the animals continued their journey. They were almost there. Just a little more to go.

SUNNY DAYS

At last, all the creatures crossed the river and made it to the meeting place. The birds, including Pete, were waiting for them. There were many plants and trees, and the area was healthy, so it was a good spot. Everyone started building their new homes. However, Sarah's mission wasn't over yet. She looked up and saw dark clouds looming on the horizon.

I have to make sure that lightning won't hit the rainforest again. Another fire would be dangerous, Sarah thought. *It's time to activate another power!*

She clapped her hands twice and said,

Bracelet, bracelet, I found you,

Show me the magic that you can do!

The screen popped up, and this time Sarah chose the power to change the weather. "Lightning, be gone!" she yelled, and pointed to the sky.

Magically, the dark clouds disappeared, and the sun was out. It was the first time the sun had come in many days. "Thank you Sarah!" the animals cheered, and started to settle in their new homes.

Sarah's mission was now complete. It was time to go home. She waved goodbye to the animals.

"Bye everyone!" she yelled. Sparkles began swirling around her. Max and Pete waved goodbye. Then, the bracelet transported her back home.

A MYSTERIOUS KEY

In a few moments, Sarah was back in her bedroom. She sat down on her bed. Even though she spent hours in the rainforest, only fifteen minutes had passed at home. Soon, Sarah noticed that her book began glowing again! New words had started appearing on the pages. She quickly started reading. They read,

Dear Sarah,

Congratulations! You have successfully completed your third mission! Keep an eye out for your next adventure. Also, remember not to tell anyone about your bracelet, or else it will disappear.

Stay safe!
-Magicland

Along with the new letter, Sarah noticed something else. There was a mysterious key. *I wonder what it could be for!* Sarah thought. What would the key unlock in Sarah's next adventures?

She sighed and drifted off to sleep.

THE END

FUN FACTS

Howler Monkeys

• Max is a howler monkey. Howler monkeys are known as one of the loudest creatures, and can be heard from up to three miles away!

• Howler monkeys can use their tails for a variety of tasks, such as hanging from tree branches.

• Howler monkeys come in many different colors. Some are a reddish color, like Max, and others can be black or a golden-brown color.

Parrots

• Parrots can come in many different sizes. The smallest parrot can be the size of your pinky, while the largest can grow up to three feet tall!

• Parrots can live for many years. The average lifespan of a parrot is 30-50 years. Interestingly, the oldest parrot was 83 years old when he passed away. That's pretty impressive!

• Parrots have a unique ability that sets them apart from other creatures; they are the only species on Earth that can mimic what humans say!

Alligators

• Male alligators are typically 11 feet long, but the longest alligator was an astonishing 19 feet long! That's equivalent to 228 inches!

• Alligators can weigh a lot. They usually weigh hundreds of pounds, and the heaviest was more than 1,000 pounds. That is an impressive weight!

• Unlike crocodiles, alligators cannot live in saltwater, and only stay in freshwater. This is the main difference between them.

The Amazon Rainforest

• The Amazon Rainforest is the largest rainforest in the world. It spans eight countries and is twice the size of India! Also, the world's second largest river, the Amazon river, runs through it. The river is more than 4,000 miles long!

• Many different animal species are found in the Amazon, and there are creatures being discovered every day! There are still many undiscovered animals and plants in the rainforest.

• The highest layer of the rainforest, known as the canopy, is so thick that it blocks out sunlight. That's why the forest floor is very dark. Also, when it rains, it takes about ten minutes for the water to reach the ground!

• The Amazon Rainforest is home to plants and animals, as well as many Native Tribes. Millions of people and other organisms call this fascinating place home.

THANKS FOR READING!

Please take a few moments to review
this book on Amazon, and stay tuned
for Sarah's next adventure!

Thanks and regards,
Aarna Agrawal

BOOKS IN THIS SERIES

The Magic Bracelet

Sarah, an adventurous eight year old girl, stumbles upon a mystical bracelet while playing in a park. She soon discovers that the bracelet can provide her with magical powers, as well as take her to exciting missions. Along the way, she encounters dangerous obstacles and many challenges, but with her quick thinking, courage, teamwork, and some help from newfound friends, she completes her missions successfully.

Sarah And The Dinosaurs

The magic bracelet takes Sarah to her first mission, an exciting adventure with the dinosaurs. A volcano is going to erupt. How will Sarah save the dinosaurs from the hot lava? Read this book to find out!

Sarah And The Dolphin

The magical bracelet has now transported Sarah into her second mission, an underwater sea adventure! She meets Pinky the dolphin and learns that a dangerous sea twister is coming. Sarah must save Pinky and her friends from the sea twister. Will she be able to save the sea animals? Dive into this magical sea adventure and enjoy reading, "The Magic Bracelet: Sarah and The Dolphin".

Made in the USA
Middletown, DE
24 April 2024

53356230R00022